Lily Takes A Walk

for
Lily

Also available in the *Spooky Surprise* series:
THE HAIRY TOE by Amelia Rosato

LILY TAKES A WALK
A PICTURE CORGI BOOK 0 552 524875
Originally published in Great Britain by Blackie and Son Ltd.

PRINTING HISTORY
Blackie edition published 1987
Picture Corgi edition published 1988

Picture Corgi Books are published by Transworld Publishers Ltd., 61-63
Uxbridge Road, Ealing, London W5 5SA, in Australia by Transworld
Publishers (Australia) Pty. Ltd., 15-23 Helles Avenue, Moorebank,
NSW 2170, and in New Zealand by Transworld Publishers (N.Z.) Ltd.,
Cnr. Moselle and Waipareira Avenues, Henderson, Auckland.

Made and printed in Portugal by Printer Portugesa.

Lily Takes A Walk

Satoshi Kitamura

A Spooky Surprise Book

A Picture Corgi

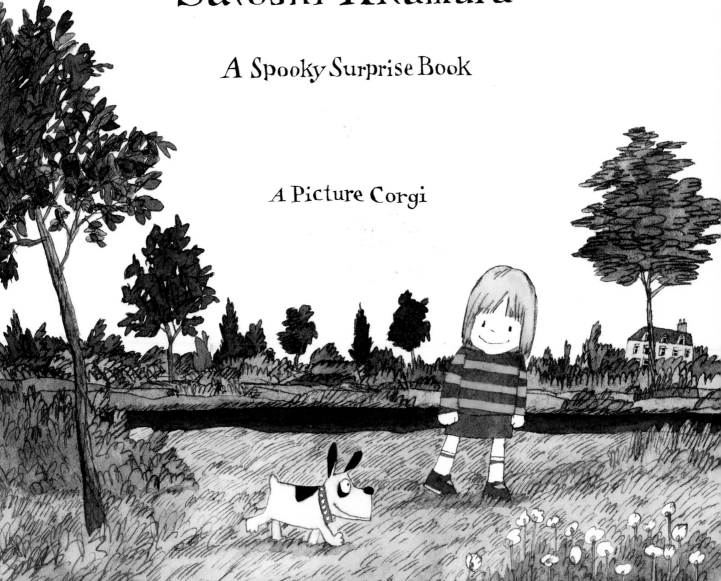

Lily likes going for walks with her dog, Nicky.

Sometimes they walk for hours and hours
until the sun starts to slip down
behind the hill.

Even if it begins to get dark on the way home,
Lily is never scared because
Nicky is there with her.

Today she does the shopping
for her mother and then...

she stops for a moment
to look at the evening star.
'Look, Nicky,' she says.
'That's called the Dog Star.'

As Lily walks past Mrs Hall's
window, she waves.
Mrs Hall is always knitting.

Bats flitter and swoop in the evening sky.
'Aren't they clever, Nicky?' says Lily. 'Not far, now.'

She stops by the bridge to say goodnight
to the gulls and the ducks on the canal.

Soon, she comes to the last corner. This is
the best moment of all. She can see
the light in her window and smell her supper cooking.

Lily's mother and father always like to hear
what she has seen on her walk.

Before long, it is time for bed.
Nicky is already in his basket.
'We had a good walk today,
didn't we?' says Lily.
'Goodnight, Nicky.
Sleep well.'